THRILL KINGS

KINGS

Convention
Collection

2

II

THRILL KINGS
Convention Collection 2

Featuring:

Not So Bad
&
The Size Of
Minneapolis Upright

By
Rik Ty

THRILL KINGS TIMELINE

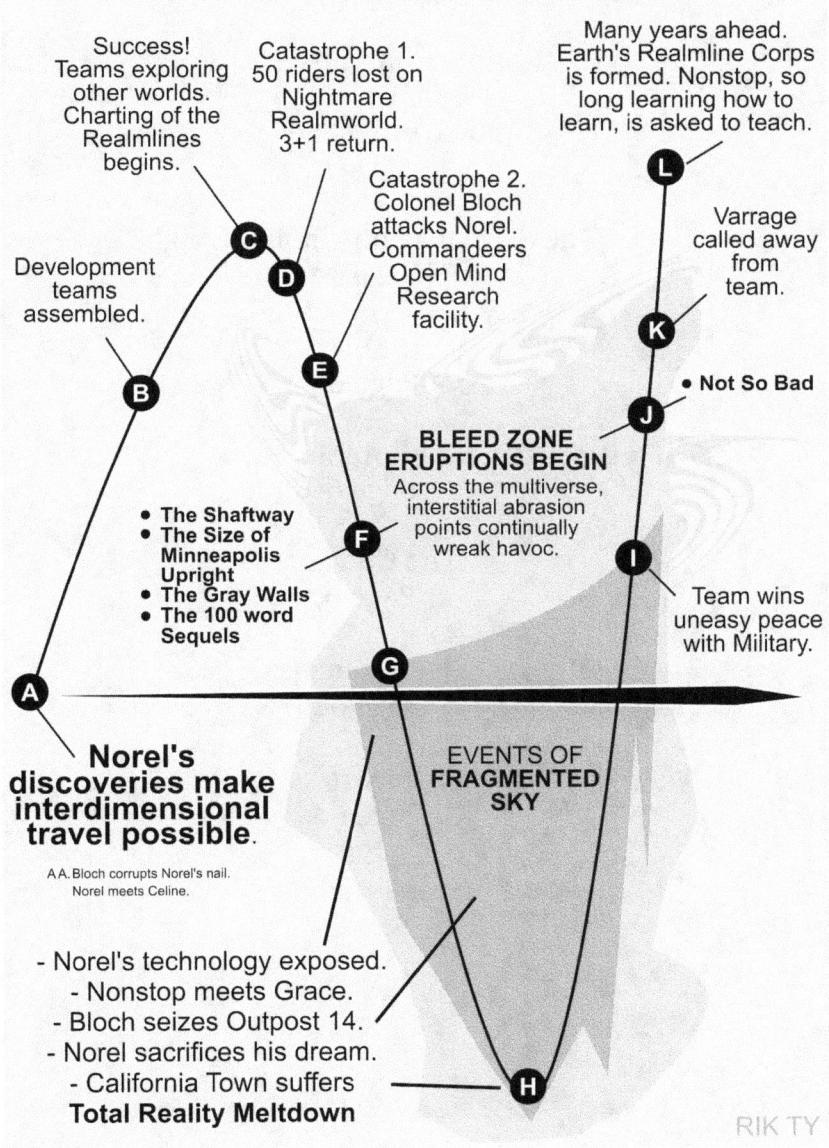

Success! Teams exploring other worlds. Charting of the Realmlines begins.

Catastrophe 1. 50 riders lost on Nightmare Realmworld. 3+1 return.

Many years ahead. Earth's Realmline Corps is formed. Nonstop, so long learning how to learn, is asked to teach.

L

Catastrophe 2. Colonel Bloch attacks Norel. Commandeers Open Mind Research facility.

Varrage called away from team.

C

D

Development teams assembled.

K

E

B

• **Not So Bad**

J

BLEED ZONE ERUPTIONS BEGIN
Across the multiverse, interstitial abrasion points continually wreak havoc.

• **The Shaftway**
• **The Size of Minneapolis Upright**
• **The Gray Walls**
• **The 100 word Sequels**

F

I

Team wins uneasy peace with Military.

G

A

Norel's discoveries make interdimensional travel possible.

EVENTS OF **FRAGMENTED SKY**

A A. Bloch corrupts Norel's nail.
Norel meets Celine.

- Norel's technology exposed.
- Nonstop meets Grace.
- Bloch seizes Outpost 14.
- Norel sacrifices his dream.
- California Town suffers **Total Reality Meltdown**

H

RIK TY

Contents:

Read By:

Date:

Thoughts:

Read By:

Date:

Thoughts:

Read By:

Date:

Thoughts:

VII

VIII

THRILL KINGS

Not
So
Bad

Rik Ty

For
Kait & Andy
May your road be smooth and easy

NONSTOP

VARRAGE

KRORK

SKYDE

DR. NOREL

GRACE

THRILL KINGS:

NOT SO BAD

Rik Ty

Dark colors swirled high in the space above his shoulders; blue tumbled into green and cascaded steadily toward the Realmlines' black horizon. Moving toward it, he watched the dark vista rise, and when its blackness split ahead of him like some biblical sea, Nonstop drove his machine onto the Earth.

He did not prolong the ride with an extended ghost. He did not resist committing. He just entered the straight clearing and noted the landscape: daylight, shoreline, ocean on his left, parkland on his right, and a cluster of buildings ahead of him at the end of a half mile or so of stony beach. He shot forward, and then moved to the side, making room for the rest of the team.

It had been a hard few weeks for our boy, and the sound of the surf was tempting. He wouldn't have minded staying right where he was, here, at the edge of the world, just watching the waves for a while.

A nice impulse, but that wasn't what his team had come for. He watched the waves for the moment he could, and then turned his head when Krork and Skyde ghosted in on the big yellow work-bike.

Krork, Nonstop's big yellow friend, smiled his big iguana-man smile, and pulled the yellow rig to a halt alongside Nonstop.

Diamondsong came through next, with Wazzi and Slice following close behind her. Wazzi and Slice drove basic vortex bikes. Diamondsong had put together a rig that looked really fun: a neon green safety cage straddling a long vortex chamber propped up on four articulated legs that each ended in a motorized wheel. She called it The Grasshopper, and Nonstop thought it looked like a blast to drive. With his own bike facing forced retirement back at base camp, part of Nonstop looked at the Grasshopper with speculative interest, but he wasn't fully ready to give up on Rattletrap yet, and so he forced himself to focus his attention on the mission at hand.

In the next second, Varrage arrived, closing out the rear, and they all took quick readings of the Bleed Zone.

Krork spoke first. He looked up from his data-box and said: "You all see it? We have a peppering of haze clusters to the west."

Diamondsong looked up and faced west. "At least that's on the inland side. That's good news. We won't have to steal any boats."

"At least not right away," Skyde joked from the truck-bike's workbay. She said this as she took the last few steps to the bike's rear gate. Then she hopped to the ground.

Nonstop stole a glance toward Diamondsong's rig. She had a passenger, Grace Peterson, who was yet another of his personal misfires from the past few weeks. Diamondsong and Grace were both misfires from his past, and he was barely two decades old. He made a point of studying his screen, though he suspected the team had moved on to another program. He didn't look up to find out.

Skyde reached under the truck-bike's workbay and slid her skyboard free. "Any good Portal candidates? Are any of those haze clusters stationary?" she asked.

"Yes," Krork said. "The Northern most cluster is big, and it isn't traveling...at the moment."

"Okay. Thanks."

Skyde stepped onto her board, synced the field locks on her boots, and began her loft. Grace stood up immediately from behind Diamondsong, with all her crazy red hair spilling out from under her helmet.

Her mirrored visor was down, a fact that Nonstop saw as a signal meaning: "Don't bother me. We're closed... All business. All day. You don't like it, Go away..." While he was peeking, Grace turned to Skyde.

"Skyde, do you have those releases?" Grace asked.

"Sure." Skyde patted a pouch on her gear harness, and changed her board's direction as she flew. "Dr Norel had no problem signing them. You want them now?"

"Yeah. I think so, before it gets too crazy."

Skyde floated closer to the rear of the Grasshopper. "Remember, you have to sign these as well. Doc included all the numbers for the lawyers," Skyde said as she handed an envelope to Grace. Diamondsong lowered the Grasshopper unit until its vortex chamber was close to the ground. Grace hopped off the back and started pulling her hover-bike free from its tow clamps. She had been sitting in its seat, and now had to get its quad pods unfolded and clicked into place.

Slice, shifting eagerly on his sleek vortex bike, nodded as he said "I have the Bleed Zone sized at about a six mile circle, getting bigger as the haze clusters run. What's the plan?"

His observation, that the Bleed Zone was getting bigger as the haze clusters ran, meant that the southern parts were moving southward, while the northern parts were moving northward and the western parts were moving westward. Which meant the Bleed Zone was a runaway train. Another runaway train.

Varrage looked up. "Skyde, check the stationary cluster. Verify that it's the portal. If it is, close it. Nonstop, go south. Get in front of the clusters and move them to the middle. Krork, go to the western-most point and do the same. I'll take the middle and deal with the inter-Ds as they show up."

Slice looked at Varrage. "What about us?"

"Stay here."

"Stay here? We came to help."

"You're civilians"

"We're all civilians."

"Stay here. If any inter-D get past me, make sure they don't run into the ocean."

"We can do more than that. Dr. Norel said we could help."

"He said you could help for an hour. But we don't know what we're dealing with, so I don't know how you can help. Right now, you are a liability. We don't know who is going to show up after the Bleed Zone is discovered. None of you are impact diffusing. None of you are bullet proof."

"We know we're not bullet proof. But we have to do something."

Grace looked back and forth between Slice and Varrage and then added Skyde to her slightly frantic gazing. "I just have an hour to get shots," she said. "I have to get shots."

"Actually, I don't mind guarding the beach," Diamondsong offered. "That sounds like a good idea."

Slice stood up fully and looked at Varrage. "How about me and Wazzi stick with Krork?"

"And I'll ride with Nonstop," Grace said, and at this, Nonstop looked up. Not closed after all.

"One hour," Varrage said. "If a single bullet flies, Wazzi, you leave. Slice you go to Grace, wherever she is. Grace, your sky-bike, it has no vortex capabilities - correct?

"Correct."

"Then Diamondsong, Slice, whoever gets to Grace first, call it in, and go. Leave the Sky-bike. Don't waste time packing it. Everybody tap."

Each member of the team unholstered their taps and did whatever was required to activate the devices. Like all their equipment, the taps were still being developed, and the optimum form for the design had yet to reveal itself. So some members pulled levers, and some activated pumps, and some unfolded hinges, and as they were ready, each member tapped the dual tips of their units against the ground and synced them with the locale's native continuum. Now all that was left for the team to do was to find out what had entered the Bleed Zone, and how they could send it home, whatever it was.

"One second everyone..." Grace said, "I'd like to get a shot of our planning stage," and as she spoke, she tossed two camera pods into the air. They blossomed, and buzzed around the group.

Varrage scowled.

Grace threw out two more.

Encouraged, Nonstop drove closer to the Grasshopper, and gave it a good look over.

"I love your rig," he said to Diamondsong.

Diamondsong re-strapped herself into her seat.

"I love it too."

"I think the little wheels across the roof are my favorite part."

"I ain't no daredevil. If I turn this thing over, I want to keep going."

"Nice Job."

"Thank you."

Nonstop turned to Grace, who was holding a single finger up to Skyde.

"Grace, what do you have in mind?" Nonstop asked.

"One second." Grace worked the cameras. They flew in fast circles around the group.

"Move out," Varrage said, and he started driving.

"Wait. Wait," Grace said, "Krork, I have to get you talking." She sent a camera to fly alongside Krork's bike, which was already moving. "Say something!"

Krork smiled at the little camera. "Hello everybody! Talk to you later." And with that, he drove off.

"Grace, good luck," Skyde said.

Grace smiled, and raised a hand high. "Vaptang," she said.

Skyde dipped her board lower, and gave Grace's hand a slow slap on the flyby. "Vaptang," she said, and she took to the sky.

Nonstop sat on his new bike, the "un-asked for" update to Rattletrap, done by professionals, and missing all of the old quirks. He had to admit, it rode like a dream. He looked at Grace. She ignored him while she gave her hover-bike the once over. He waited while she did, deliberately calm, deliberately dis-mindful to a host of pressures: his new bike, Grace's new priorities, a runaway train to deal with — a world that never held still. Nope. It never did. And add to that, the fact that the world just blended up with twenty million other worlds, none of which held still either, and you had a pretty good idea of the constant state of, oh just forget it. What's everyone else doing?

Grace got herself strapped in, looked up, and gave Nonstop a little wave and a little smile. Then she started the quiet engines, and the bike's propellers sliced the air, adding their own whisper to the mix. Grace lofted the bike frame a few feet off the ground, and spoke. "Nonstop, I don't imagine I can keep up with you," she said. "But the cameras should be able to. I can be a little more daring with them."

"It's nice that we'll be teaming up."

"You're the wild rider. You're where the best shots will be."

"Oh," Nonstop said, then added, "You know it."

"You have your data box on? You have it set on bleed-band?" she asked, and as her voice came out of the data box clipped to his belt, she had her answer.

"You bet. I'm heading for those buildings, and the roads next to them."

Nonstop spun on the bike's great big, round single wheel, the reason everyone called the rig "8-ball", and headed for the boardwalk.

He was already used to its grip system, two ski-pole things with controls in the hand units. The rig had a cross bar grip down by the display. It was a lot like Rattletrap, except the arm systems were fused to the vortex chamber, not swinging around like a second torso. This put the center of gravity right under his feet, and he had to admit that was awesome!

As Nonstop sped up, 8-Ball sounded the jungle-cat noise. This surprised Nonstop a little, but he hadn't turned the feature off, and so it shouldn't have. But, he wondered, did 8-ball deserve a jungle-cat noise? He had installed the gimmick on Rattletrap for fun, and the team had replicated the feature, but did it belong on the new bike?

Rattletrap was a machine.

Rattletrap was JUST a machine.

It didn't matter which bike had the jungle-cat noise, or if they both did. It wasn't a betrayal. You couldn't betray a machine.

He shut the feature off with a slap and had the bike lift its parkour arms, also upgraded by the professionals back at the lab, who, with the best of intentions, and with unmistakable enthusiasm, had taken his design ideas, and shown him how they should actually be done. But the bike was awesome. He could feel its potential thrumming in its moves, waiting for his reluctance to morph into lust.

But Rattletrap was his buddy, wasn't he? Machine or not? And it felt like the bike had died in his arms. When Nonstop passed through that cloud, and later, when the rust-fever hit the bike, and every moving part on Rattletrap had seized shut, it really had felt like the bike had died.

Krork had helped him. They put Rattletrap in the truck bike's workbay as if it were an ambulance, and drove the bike back to basecamp. And now Rattletrap's restoration was a spare time activity, and who had spare time?

8-ball grooved up the stony beach, grinding and crackling its tire on the long strait-away.

"Grace, how you doin'?" Nonstop asked.

Grace leaned forward in her safety harness, tilting the hover-bike and its four propellers forward, gaining both altitude and speed.

"Everything's fine. I'm on your six. Doing good. I'm hot under the kevlar, but the airflow is cooling. I'm good. Are we headed any place specific?"

"Just doing a loose curve south. I'm going to head off the furthest cluster, and if it's a creature, I'm going to try to get it to move to the center."

"All right. I'll let you know if I see anything interesting."

Nonstop neared the end of the beach. A pier stood ahead of him, chest high, leading to a boardwalk and some shops.

He sped up, and decided to give 8-ball a slightly more aggressive field test than he had so far. He made 8-ball hold out its arms, and when they reached the pier, he skimmed the walkway for a fraction of a second, then lifted, rolled, and hopped the bike up onto the pier. He wobble-spun on the big round tire after a bounce, and as the bike twirled forward, he revved into a straight away. He grabbed a light pole with the bike's arms, used it to spin, and vaulted up onto the roof of the first storefront — an ice cream parlor that also sold sun glasses. The shop was deserted. So was the boardwalk.

The roof was long, shared by many stores, and as Nonstop sped along it, Grace raced forward to catch up to him.

"Are you just going to send the creatures to the center? Or are you going to try and send them home?"

"Oh yeah, if we find them, we'll try to send them home. If that works, great. The trick is to try from an angle that steers them even if it doesn't do the whole job."

"There's a trick?"

"Yeah, you shoot the side opposite the direction you want them to go."

Nonstop tried a shoulder roll back off the building, but the new bike didn't have enough distance between its shoulder plane and its fuselage. He had to slap one of the robot arms down to prevent the move from slamming his head into the rooftop. Airborne, he positioned the bike for a full wheel landing, and bounced into his course correction, hitting the asphalt of the city street, and making a bee-line for the corner, and the first of a series of right turns.

Grace, flying above the tree-line, had no problem keeping up with him, though she lost sight of him here and there as she hunted through the tree branches for flashes of his orange bike, or the red on the hoodie he was wearing.

Alone on her flying bike, she found it stressful trying to keep Nonstop in sight, but nowhere near as stressful as trying to avoid him usually was; him and his constant energy. Maybe this was her answer: just make him the subject of every project, and then he couldn't interrupt her work with offers of fun. Great. Fifteen thousand universes to explore, and as long as every story was about Nonstop, she could have peace. That sounded splendid. Yes. That would be just wonderful.

As she looked for Nonstop, she lost sight of the landscape, and the next time she viewed it, she got a surprise.

"Nonstop! I see something! a few streets up, there's a dust cloud coming."

Nonstop looked at 8-ball's display, like Rattletrap's, on the visible side of the arms' engine pod.

"I see the haze cluster coming. But not the dust. Oh wait..."

"Oh-MY- G - Nonstop, it's like a giant octopus!"

"What?"

"I just saw it for a second. It jumped up, and then slipped below the tree line again."

"Well, now its heading west. Did it see you?"

"I don't know. Maybe. You think it's running?"

"Yeah."

And with that, the giant pink octo-monster breached the treeline again with a leap, and this time, Grace saw the back of its head. Big. Massive. With a surface that seemed to waver and flutter slightly from its own movement. For the instant she saw it, the creature's head looked like a giant, partially-inflated-parade-balloon. Either that, or a giant, pink tonsil.

And then it was gone again.

"Yeah, he's running."

"Okay, we're going to stay on his left and try to get in front of him," Nonstop said. He gave the bike some juice and tripled its speed.

"When I catch up to it, I'm going to hit it with tap and try to send it home. You're ready with your camera things, right?"

"Yeah. Don't worry about the cameras. Just do your thing like I'm not here."

Grace sped up as she answered, but fell behind. She sent two cameras ahead of her, but they couldn't keep up with Nonstop either. Ten seconds behind him turned to two minutes behind him, and finally five before her cameras found him again. She

14

could see some mayhem on her screens, and she could see some mayhem with her own eyes, just by looking up.

Far off, she saw the octo-monster leap onto a peaked roof, gallop over it with ropy, folded legs, straighten its legs to their full length and leap off the roof, gaining massive amounts of distance. Nonstop shot up the same roof, launched it like a ramp, arced over to a tree, swung the bike from a branch, over to another tree, swung from another branch, landed on a long flat roof, drove it at high speed, and had the motorcycle cartwheel over the edge and down to the street below, where Grace lost sight of him again. Rather than chase after Nonstop, Grace opted for height. She kept a general idea of where Nonstop was, but up high, she saw dust clouds all over town, most with leaping pink centers, The town looked like a giant griddle filled with weird fried eggs. What would it take to get one single creature isolated and what would they miss in the meantime?

Grace decided to make a small adjustments to her shots. She called back one of the cameras, and synced it with the hover bike's own cameras to set up coverage that would suggest the full scope of the Bleed Zone the team was dealing with, or at least what she could see of it. Where was Nonstop? Camera two was keeping up with him. Camera three was on Krork, but showed debris on the lens. Move camera four from Slice to Krork, call back camera three to clean manually. Where was Nonstop? There. Good. Shot D on the back burner for now. Shot A, shot B, shot C. All good. Go. Go.

On the street, Nonstop was piecing together a better look at the inter-D. It was as big as an elephant and then some, and it looked more like an octopus than anything else, but it had fat legs and thin legs, spurs and tusks and thick patches of hide. It looked like a bag of beet roots, or a wine-colored mop.

Big as it was, it was surprisingly fast. Nonstop saw it grab a tree in one tentacled arm, and hoist itself over a house. Nonstop

15

might be able to follow it, but not in one move. He revved for the tree, spotted a crowd of people standing inside a coffee shop doorway, and then grabbed the tree. He launched to a peaked roof, drove up and over it, looked for traces of — There! — a glimpse of <u>pink</u> Goliath on the other side of some trees, already behind another block of houses.

So, same deal.

Nonstop bounced along the street, grabbed a light-pole, and vaulted to another peaked roof. Over it easily, he landed on the next street, and sped after the monster, gaining ground on the flat road, and aiming his tap at the creature as he drew nearer.

He pressed the trigger. A distortion beam rippled the air between his tap and the monster, buzzing with spots of blue light where it connected with the creature. Instantly, the monster reached up to a chimney with one arm to change direction, paffed open like some kind of giant sunflower or beach umbrella, and then cartwheeled itself right-ward, neatly rolling itself up and over the gray peaked roof attached to the chimney.

"Air brakes!" Nonstop said aloud. "Slick."

Nonstop straight-armed the bike into a gymnast's side spin and rolled up the nearest roof. He reached the other side already firing, blasting tap-beam right where the creature was running.

It wasn't working. The creature wasn't turning blue or fading home.

The creature grabbed a tree trunk and spun toward the gap between two houses. Nonstop took the same turn and followed, hitting the creature with tap the whole way. The creature reached a tree-lined intersection between houses, and stopped quickly. It pulled in its arms, and started spinning like a top. As Nonstop entered the open space, the creature let several arms out again, smacking Nonstop at least twice as it sent him flying.

Nonstop reacted by skipping into a sidelong drift-turn. Then he stabilized, and shot forward, still firing tap.

And still getting no result.

The octopus pulled itself up into a tree, leapt to another tree, and swung to a third. Nonstop struggled just to keep the creature in sight, let alone within his jerking tap beam.

The creature rolled over another roof, and out of sight. Nonstop followed using a straight path between two houses, and as he drove, he spoke loudly into the air. "Hey Eyebird, can you hear me?"

"You mean me?" Grace asked over the data-box.

"Yeah, Grace, sorry, I mean you." He glimpsed the creature turning a corner, and steered toward it, lowering his tap. "I wanna trap this guy long enough to send him home. Right now, he's too big and too fast. You have the high view. Can you see any dead end streets I can lead it to?"

"Dead ends, you mean like a cul de sacs?"

"Maybe. What's a cul de sac?"

"It's like a round street in front of houses. Like a courtyard - but a street."

"Oh sure, I know those things. Sure, that's what I meant. That. Are there any?"

"I'll check, let me pull up."

"Yes, I think I see a bunch of them, though it looks like there are plenty of gaps between the houses. Wait. I see a good one. There's a motel complex like a big half circle."

"Yeah? Great."

"There's a gas station way ahead of you, two blocks past that, you go right, and after a bunch of blocks, the street ends at the motel."

"Got it. What's the name of the gas station?"

"Uhm, uh, uhhhhhm ... Villa, also, Villa Pete's Auto Care is what the sign says on the little side building."

"Got it, thanks!" Nonstop said, and Grace watched him hook a fast left.

"What? The gas station is straight..." she asked herself. "Where's he go... Oh yeah. Right. the monster.

*

Nonstop tried a fast haze reading with his databox, but couldn't refine the search while driving. Taking the haze reading with the bike would offer a bigger screen, but he'd have to slow down to even try it. Suddenly, he worried that touching the databox had cost him the bleed-band connection. He tried the connection.

"Grace can you hear me? Can you see the Inter-D? I've lost him."

Relieved, he heard Grace say, "Sure. I'll fly a little higher..."

Grace lofted. As she began her lift, she considered sending a camera out to aid in the search, but found that she didn't need to.

"Yes, Nonstop. I see it. Its about eight blocks ahead of you to the right. On your 2."

"Dig it. Thank you. Okay, same as before, I'm going to swing in front and start steering the creature to that block with the motel."

With speed his only objective, Nonstop blazed impressively. What Grace could see of him quickly diminished with distance, but surprisingly, his voice came through her data box as if he were standing right next to her. The mis-match was mildly unsettling, and Grace felt distracted as Nonstop's voice continued: "Grace, I'm driving a bit blind — will you help me fine tune when I get closer to him?"

"Yes, absolutely," she answered him. "Keep doing what you're doing. You want to keep the monster in the space between you and the motel, right?"

"Right. It should run away from me, and wind up running to the motel. How tall is the motel?"

"Tall in places, but small in places too."

"Yeah, this guy can hop over roofs. I need him..."

"Nonstop, you're close to it now. If you make your next right, it would be two blocks away."

"All right. Thanks. I have to over shoot."

"Nonstop, what if I flew at the roof of the motel? Would that keep the creature from hopping over the roof?"

"That is a great idea! Can you get there?"

"Yes. If I go now."

"Cool. I'll find this guy, and eventually get him to run where we want him. But Grace, don't be obvious. If he sees you above the motel, he might not go down that block. Try and stay out of sight until I'm tapping him good and solid."

"You got it."

*

Grace checked her cameras, saw that each transmission was flowing fine, and actually turned away from the action. Flying over the local streets was suddenly interesting in a new way. It was kind of fun. She did see a few people peeking out of doorways. She saw more than one person point at her as she passed. Many people were out driving their cars, as if they didn't know anything was going on. Maybe they didn't. Before she even realized she was doing it, she flew low through the next intersection, low enough to be seen by drivers - hopefully, a strange enough sight to put them on their guard, to break them out of complacency. The worry that she might have gotten hit by a quickly approaching truck only occurred to her later.

Up the next street, she flew higher. She checked her cameras. The one behind Nonstop showed hints of pink monster, slipping in and out of the frame. She'd have to go faster.

*

19

Nonstop followed behind the octo-monster, slow enough to avoid overtaking it, fast enough to keep the creature moving. He let it pull ahead, hoping that when they reached the motel, he might catch it confused, catch it looking for a gap along the front of the building. Then a long enough tap would send it home, and they could move on to the next creature. Nonstop slowed, and watched the inter-D enter the last block.

When it did, he sped forward, cameras buzzing around him, and then, he too entered the courtyard, tap ready, —

— and suddenly he had to dive the bike along the ground as an uprooted tree rocketed toward his head, roots first, spewing dirt like a black comet. He slid under the missile, with the camera drones whizzing right alongside him. Then a rain of dirt blasted him as the flying tree obliterated a standing motel sign. The tree landed in the street, its leaves and branches hissing against the asphalt as it slowed to a stop.

The cameras caught it all. Hovering behind the motel, Grace saw it on her monitor, and as soon as she saw that Nonstop wasn't hurt, she flagged the shots for later inspection; a loop of Nonstop getting showered with dirt might be good for a highlight reel.

Nonstop came out of the slide firing, but there was nothing in the courtyard left to hit.

He watched as a last bit of tentacle slipped past a chimney, and then he followed.

"Nonstop, we missed it. Are you okay?"

"I'm fine. I probably would have been fine even if it hit me," Nonstop said as he sped for one of the motel's lower roofs. He used the bike's arms to spring vault over the roof's rain gutters, and sped up its shingles.

"That didn't work at all," he said. "All we did was teach it a new trick. Throwing trees - dag."

Nonstop waved at Grace as he cleared the roof, his body communicating with her visually, while his voice continued a different conversation through the device on her belt — weird. "Grace, we're lucky he didn't throw a tree at you! Dig it, Varrage is right. If this bug decides to clobber you, you don't have any impact diffusion, and..." Nonstop cleared the roof, and Grace couldn't see him anymore.

*

Nonstop dropped down the other side of the building, ready to fire, aiming his tap... at nothing. The street offered only yards and fences and trashcans.

"Grace do you see it?"

"No. The cameras are searching, but no. I'm heading higher."

Nonstop coasted forward. He touched his data box, but then released it.

"Wait," Grace's voice said. "I see it. It stopped. Three blocks to your left, on your 10."

"Thanks, you see it, or the cameras see it?"

"The cameras."

"Does it have a tree?"

"Uhhhh, Yes! Nonstop, it's holding two trees."

"Dag, we're gonna do this all day."

He looked down the street. Sunlight glared off windows. It also brightened a row of treetops.

"Nonstop, can you call in Krork?"

"Yeah. Maybe. Maybe we should double team these guys and get rid of them one at a time."

Nonstop coasted toward the corner. "Let me try something," he said.

He worked at the controls on the hand grips, trusting that if the result wasn't exactly what he had in mind, he could adjust.

21

He pressed the switch,

The new bike made a blatty engine noise, like a traditional motorcycle.

Pretty good. It could stand to be a little louder, so... one more adjustment brought it into line, and Nonstop advanced to the corner, traveling very slowly and very loudly. He started down the next empty street.

"Grace, how did the creature react? Did it do anything?"

"It flinched, yeah, but it didn't run. It raised one of the trees."

"Okay, thanks. Let me know if it leaves," Nonstop continued down the streets — engine noises slow and loud, puttering and coughing.

When he approached the end of the last street, he moved close to the corner of the last house, the last spot where he was still hidden from the creature. He reached out an arm and waved.

"Anything, Grace?"

"Yes. It's looking at you."

"The tree?"

"Very high. He's ready to nail you."

"Let me know if he lowers it."

Nonstop made lowering motions with his arm, his hand palm-side down. After a moment, Grace let him know the monster had lowered the trees... slightly.

Nonstop trundled out from hiding, lowering the noise of the bike, and emerging just in time to see the octi slip away between two houses.

It was gone.

But it had left the trees.

Nonstop trundled around the uprooted maples, and as he did, he saw a group of people at a second floor window, looking stunned. He waved. The adults waved back slowly. The kids waved back wildly. He followed the octi, his bike still puttering engine noise.

"Grace, do you have him? Let me know which way he goes. I want to stay back and out of sight."

"Sure," Grace said, and she led Nonstop with cues of "Right" or Left", or "It slipped into the alley," types of comments. It was an easy few minutes. Nonstop simply let it be known that he was following the creature, but not speeding up to catch it. Just staying even. Nonstop even started to enjoy the ride; 8-ball's front anchored suspension worked great. He felt the breeze and noticed the sun dappling through the trees.

He came to a corner, and saw the creature pause in an intersection two blocks away. The creature looked at Nonstop. Nonstop waved with his whole arm, but didn't speed up. The creature ran. Nonstop followed.

He crossed another avenue, and caught a glimpse of a black SUV crossing the same avenue several blocks away, moving in the same direction he was. Civilians? Government guys? Army?

A building blocked his view of the SUV, and he continued following the creature.

After a few moments of following down blocks and turning corners, he came to a large intersection, and found the creature poised over toward the right side of the street, standing with its legs spread wide so that it was only half its full height. It rested there panting, looking at Nonstop.

Nonstop stopped, and they stood there for a moment, both of them just looking. Nonstop waved with one hand and lowered his tap with the other. The creature waved too. Where was Krork, his friend, the linguistic chameleon? Here was the moment for communication, but Nonstop himself had no translation skills to offer.

Rather than just stand there gaping. Nonstop pointed to the creature, and pantomimed swinging from tree to tree, and then he looked to the sky and made a blowing-up gesture with the full reach of both his arms.

23

He didn't know if the creature understood his attempt at expressin — admiration, but he thought the creature seemed pleased — maybe. It remained calm in any case. Then it did something surprising. It pointed down the block, and when Nonstop turned, he saw a lighthouse, blocks and blocks away.

Nonstop looked back at the creature, and the creature imitated Nonstop's tree to tree gesture — remarkably well. The creature pointed at the trees on one side of the street, then at the other side of the street, and pantomimed swinging from branch to branch. It would have been right at home on a dance floor.

And then the creature pointed at Nonstop and at itself.

Nonstop laughed hard. He actually held his belly, and threw back his head, and something washed over him like a tonic. He looked at the creature.

"Ohhhh, you want to do a run? Or a race? Aces!" Nonstop said, and his spirit lifted. He waved and smiled. He holstered his tap, and pointed to his hand.

"Nonstop, what are you doing?" Grace asked over the data box, but close enough to be heard with Nonstop's ears alone. Nonstop turned, and saw Grace hovering at a corner, just out of the monster's sight, but watching the scene play out on her monitor.

"Looks like we're going to have a little fun," Nonstop said, turning back to the creature. He held up three fingers, and pointed at them with his free hand. Then he dropped the fingers one by one, and followed that move by making a zooming motion with his whole arm, pointing his hand at the lighthouse. Instantly, the creature seemed to understand. It held up three tentacle tips, curled them one by one, and then made a zooming motion toward the lighthouse with all three arms.

A race then.

Maybe.

Sort of.

"Grace, I think this sand crab wants to race."

"Send it home."

"I will, I will. But this could be cool."

"It could be a trap. It could be waiting to kill you."

"There are easier ways to do that - tree smashing for one, hundred arm strangling for another. Waiting in the middle of the street isn't sneaky. There's that, at least."

"You're going to play along? Boy, you take a lot of chances."

"Nah..." Nonstop said, and he swung into position on his side of the intersection, more or less even with the creature's large head, and hopefully, more than a tentacle's distance from its body. With a serviceable starting line established, he looked at the creature.

The creature adjusted perfectly, as if its understanding of the situation was in complete alignment with Nonstop's.

The creature raised three tentacles. Nonstop smiled hugely, and held up three fingers. They both began the countdown, and took off for the lighthouse, followed by Grace, and a pair of her flying camera drones.

The monster started a slap-gallop-snake-slide along its many legs, and Nonstop reached the trees first. He vaulted high, hooked a first branch on the down arc, and swung the bike though the air, headed for the next tree.

Then the creature reached a tentacle to its first tree, and that was it! It contracted the arm. pulled itself skyward, and back-spun its whole body in a high-air somersault. The creature sailed over the neighboring tree, reached for a branch on the tree beyond that, and re-launched into the air with a grand, open spin that looked like a twirling umbrella. The move displayed flares of orange in the skin between the creature's magenta tentacles. It spun to the next tree, and the next tree, and the next, then galloped up the bricks of a five story building before attempting to leap across a wide street to the next block of buildings; a distance that included four driving lanes, two parking lanes, and two sidewalks.

The creature almost cleared the entire avenue. It landed in the street, with its legs progressing in a jerky-gallop of high, tentacle stilt-shapes, moves that kept the creature's head descending gently as it rocketed to the next line of trees.

Nonstop switched to merely driving along the street, momentarily abandoning the swinging ride-idea in favor of just watching the creature make its moves.

One of the camera drones circled him, and then buzzed forward. Nonstop sped to catch up with the creature, and when he did, he leapt the bike into the tree behind it, following the creature's moves, arcing from the same branches, flipping when it flipped. The creature, seeing this, traded the quest for speed for the quest for artistry, twining deeper into the tree structures, and changing directions with dazzling moves. The creature's head, when not compressed, was larger than Nonstop's new bike, so the path it led, while dizzying, was one Nonstop could follow.

The incentive to get with the flow made Nonstop sensitive to the new bike's handling in a way he had been reluctant to approach. But reading the bike, responding to its balance, and its reach, and its re-positionings, was necessary if he hoped to keep up with the free runner ahead of him.

Grace flew closer to Nonstop.

"You both look absolutely crazy," she said.

Nonstop glanced up, yelled "Aces!" and then looked forward again.

"Nonstop, when do we send it home?"

"After the run! It's big, and it won't hold still. There's too much mass to move with a glancing shot. We have to let it tire itself out."

Grace watched as the cephalopod cartwheeled into the air: a sunburst of orange and magenta that slipped down into a tree and pinwheeled skyward again spectacularly.

"Letting it tire itself out...Is that's what we're doing? Looks more like you're just having fun," she said. "And there are like 30 of these things; how are we going to tire them all out?"

"One at a time I guess, Krork has a bigger tap, and Varrage's bike can become a bigger tap. That will help. And there are eight of us, and Krork has some back-up taps in his rig. We could get you in on the action, and we could deputize some regular people too. I don't know, but this feels like a positive, and I'm going to trust my gut."

"You're talking yourself into something because you want it to be true, not because it is."

Nonstop followed the inter-D in serpentines along the ground. Grace serpentined right alongside him in the dappled light under the trees.

"You might be right. But he's inviting me on a run, and I'm taking him up on it. Maybe what's next is what ever we make next."

"Oh. THAT sounds familiar. What are we actually talking about here, Nonstop?"

"Don't worry. I'm talking about the Bleed Zone. You and me are cool. I got it. You need space to work. That I know. What I don't know is what I'm going to do with jiggly-head here... but I know I can't do nothing."

A few trees ahead, the monster spun a loop around a branch and stole a glance at Nonstop's position. Nonstop sped up.

"Nonstop, it's a monster."

"It's not a monster. It's a dude."

"Ugh. There we go again — right away assuming that it's male. So charming."

27

"I have no idea if its a male, or a female, or a whatever — it's a dude, though."

"Hmmph. The Captain of the Patriarchy speaks again."

"It's not the patriarchy. It's my default. I'm entitled to my default the same as everybody else."

"Your default? Where'd you pick up that idea?"

"From Krork. When I asked him what the "patriarchy' was. I'm losing the mo, Grace. I can't really discuss this right now."

"That's because I'm right."

"Huh? No, look, maybe, I don't know. I can't drive well and talk well. - What do you see on the ..."

"Nonstop, it could grab you by the ankles and bash your brains out."

"I think we're past that."

"You think? So what? Who cares what you think? It could kill you."

"Man oh man, I have to accept all the bad things. I don't want to refuse all the good things too. This feels like a good thing."

"We have to send it home."

"We'll send it home when it flat-lines."

"You'll be flat-lining too. What if it decides to eat you for a pick-me-up?"

"Ahhhh, that's right. I'm fast-food — quickest snack there is..." Nonstop said, speeding up.

Grace grunted and lofted the hover bike higher, checking the feeds from the drones she had flanking, or at least trying to flank, the speedy inter-D.

She watched as Nonstop caught up to the creature, and they expanded their run to include light poles and awnings and fire escapes, zig-zagging their way nearer to the beach. Then she heard voices coming over her data box, and she saw Nonstop slow down.

*

Nonstop's data box lit up on his belt. Krork's voice came through.

"Nonstop, I see a haze cluster heading toward that light house - is that you?"

Nonstop gripped the box, and spoke loudly.

"Yeah, I'm on it."

"I've got an inter-D still running ahead of me, also heading toward the light house. I'm west of you."

Nonstop glanced up, and saw the weak dust cloud coming over the rooftops.

"I think I see you. Krork. Listen, these creatures are smart. They're not just big animals. Me and the one I'm chasing are kind of just playing. Maybe we can get them to hold still voluntarily. Have you spoken to them yet?"

"No, not yet. No opportunity. I can't catch them. And I haven't been able to send any to Varrage either. Have you?"

"No. To tell you the truth, I forgot all about Varrage. Something kind of good is starting here, though. It should involve you — a little sign language communication you can build on. I'll see you at the light house. Maybe we can make something happen."

Something happened right then, long before the lighthouse. The second monster, bright green and brilliant, thundered out from a side street. It galloped into an intersection a block ahead, and slapped a pirouette in the intersection's center. The octi Nonstop was following leapt out of its tree and cartwheeled down the street toward the other monster. The two monsters met, entwined, and flung each other along the street.

Nonstop sped to catch up.

Were they fighting?

Were they wrestling?

Despite the ferocity of each hurl, no damage seemed to be being done to either creature, or to the town. They seemed to be using each other for momentum and nothing more. Nonstop swerved closer as the camera drones whizzed and wove around the flailing cephalopods.

The house-lined streets gave way to business-lined streets, all heading for a grand, paved pavilion that led to the start of the stony beach.

Nonstop swung past the creatures and beat them to the paved concourse. As he drove alongside its low wall, the magenta octi landed in the pavilion's center — alone. The light green monster slipped to the rim wall and perched there. Nonstop circled the magenta creature, and it spun in time with him, keeping them both facing each other. Then it held out two thin tentacles, and sent one to sway directly in front of Nonstop. It sent the other to sway directly behind him. Neither arm touched Nonstop. Both just kept pace.

Were they dancing? Was this a bullfight?

Nonstop, not feeling completely in control, decided to test. He hop-spun on his giant round tire and cut backwards on the third bounce. As the octi reacted to keep its arms pacing with Nonstop, Nonstop moved again, but then slowed, so the octi could re-position. Then the octi surprised Nonstop. It draped five large tentacles across the pavement in front of Nonstop, and kept them in position as Nonstop drove. The octi spun, matching Nonstop, and the large arms started to look like a banking curve, complete with a safety rail.

Nonstop glanced at the octi's eyes. Then he pointed at the curving arms, and the octi pointed too. Nonstop sped up, started up the arms, and the creature instantly rose and shifted, supplying Nonstop with other curving paths to ride along.

Grace arrived near them, keeping to the air, stunned by what she was seeing. Nonstop drove along the arms of the creature, not

30

rushing, and as each pathway was crossed, the monster provided a new pathway of curved arms to ride. A dance. Motion for the sake of motion.

Grace piloted the camera drones, and made them circle from opposite directions. swirling in an orbit around Nonstop while her hover-bike caught the stationary view. The stream she was capturing was the most fluid and exciting thing she had ever even tried to catch with a camera, and while she was busy, the green octi slapped its way down to the beach.

Skyde arrived on the skyboard and circled overhead; Krork pulled up on the big yellow bike and parked on a sidewalk. He trotted over to Grace, laughing at the Statue of Liberty-flamenco dance Nonstop and the octi appeared to be doing. "That's a first," Krork said, and he watched as Nonstop drove up an extended arm into the sunlight, spun a slow 360 at the top of the arm and spiraled back down into a great knot of tentacles.

A loud clacking sound came from the beach. The green octi stood high, bobbing its head as it watched every move Nonstop made, tapping one stone against another to get its friend's attention, making curved lanes out of its own arms as well.

"Does it want to play catch?" Grace asked, and with that, the magenta creature rippled over to the pavilion wall, and threw Nonstop high. The arc was smooth and gentle, more like a toss than a throw, and the green octi caught Nonstop without a pause in the flow.

Krork watched each point of contact, frowning slightly. "That's our boy they're flinging around."

"He's loving it," Grace said as she landed the hover bike on the ground. "At least he seems to be. Hey Nonstop! You're making us nervous. Get them to play catch with something that isn't you!"

"What? Things are fine!" Nonstop's voice said over the data box.

"Can't you all play catch with your safety rope, or your sword, or your harness?"

"What?"

"I'll find something," Krork said. "He'll never be able to rig something up driving like that. Let him concentrate."

Grace looked at Krork, who smiled and left.

"Nonstop. Never mind. Just be safe." Grace added.

Nonstop waved, and drove, and flipped, and cartwheeled amid the moving arms of the creatures. He steered to the ground, and drove in long lazy circles, and the two creatures alternated between making room for him to ride, and making ramps for him to climb. He took one of them, and the lazy circles moved back to the air.

Each of the octi used a lesser arm to hold a small stone, and together, began tapping out a beat.

More octi showed up on the beach, steadily, until ALL the octi showed up on the beach. In seconds, the creatures surrounded the two inter-D that were dancing with Nonstop, and began joining in -- if not in the dance, then in the stone tapping. The rhythm grew loud. Each stone offered its own particular note, and the tapping took on a buzzing quality as the different notes coalesced and found each other. Then the rhythm turned into music. Not Earth music maybe, not music based on 4 beats per measure, but music based on a more complex number, one that incorporated 4, and one the humans could find a beat in that they liked anyway.

The music called the townspeople. They drew nearer, tentative at first, but then bolder. At the awesome site of gigantic, colorful, outer-space octo-monsters dancing on their shoreline, several older kids ran forward.

One kid came bounding out from the crowd ... "Wait, wait," he yelled, holding up a black can with speaker grids on its ends.

"Yo Hector, drop some beats!" someone yelled from the crowd. And the kid did just that, blasting his groove, and rushing in among the creatures like a double-dutcher leaping into a jump-rope session.

The octis kept their music steady, but seemed to enjoy the new music as well, adjusting their bopping and swaying to match the new music more closely. The town's kids started dancing too.

Varrage pulled up alongside Grace. and Grace did her best not to flinch at his grim appearance, his faceted, obsidian skin, the roiling, yellow gap that held his facial features, the lips that did not smile. Varrage said nothing, but stood, and looked on at the alien crowd, and at Nonstop swinging around between them.

"What do you know about the creatures?" Varrage asked Grace without looking at her.

"Nonstop says they're smart. They seem to like acrobatics. They defend themselves."

"I heard some of that over the data box. This is what he meant by 'smart'?" Varrage asked, then he backed his bike up, drove away from the pavilion, and changed direction at the first corner.

Over the data box, Grace heard Krork call for Skyde, and she watched as Skyde changed directions in the air. Skyde descended toward a storefront a block away, where Krork was standing, holding out a colorful beach bag by a long strap.

Krork tossed the bag up to Skyde. They spoke briefly, and then Skyde flew her board nearer to Nonstop, dangling the colorful canvas bag by its bright orange strap, and swinging it as she approached.

"Nonstop! Catch!" She said loudly, tossing the bag high.

Nonstop gave her a thumbs up, and caught the bag. He glimpsed that as soon as Skyde passed over the octi, they froze, even retracted a little, and suddenly Nonstop had to reach out with the bike's arms and swing a trapeze move off the Green octi's tentacles. Every octi Skyde passed froze as she moved over it. She darted sideways to get away from them, and they moved freely as soon as she gained some distance.

Nonstop noticed, but didn't comment. Instead, he tossed the bag high in the air.

"What's in it?" he asked over the data box as the octi grabbed the bag and started the catch session.

"Blankets!" Skyde answered back, as she circled overhead, away from the creatures.

Nonstop played along too, catching the bag and flinging it skyward. The creatures gave him rampways to ride, and tossed the bag where he might catch it. Each time he missed, one of the creatures caught the bag, or one of the humans on the beach took a turn. It never hit the ground.

Krork approached Grace as she filmed Nonstop and the crowd.

"Much better," he said.

Grace stopped, looked at Krork, and smiled.

"That was nice how you stepped in to find that bag," she said.

"Well, I had some band-width to spare. I'm not doing MY specialty at the moment, and that's a good time to help. Where did Varrage go?"

"I don't know. Doing his specialty, I'd guess."

Krork looked around him, and added, "Hmmm."

*

Varrage reached the stony beach and drove toward the shoreline. He turned his twin tailed bike at the crowd of dancing inter-D, smacked his tap against the ground, and inserted the device into a dock on the back of the bike. The twinned vortex chambers began to glow.

A purple octi broke away from the crowd of creatures on the beach, larger than the rest, thicker, and heavier, sporting plenty of tusks.

The octi approached Varrage, quickly and purposefully. It raised several of its tentacles, thick, and thin, and made itself look huge, like a dark sunburst speeding down the beach.

Varrage pivoted his bike, and pointed its rear at the nearing creature. The creature stopped, but loomed.

Varrage could see that the creature's hide was thick and cracked and dusty. The skin along its major legs was textured with rigid wedges that looked like motocross tread. Of the massive legs the creature held high, it moved two of the thinnest. It folded the first into a rough, club shape, then positioned the second into a horizon line with a slim, single fold that protruded at a right angle. The fold could have represented a nail in a board, or a man on a beach.

The octi brought down the club-arm, and pantomimed flattening the protrusion.

Varrage, a man whose strangely healed, dimensionally wounded skin, resembled volcanic rock atop glowing lava, raised his strange arms, tensed his glowing fingers, and brought his open hands to their opposing elbows. Openly displaying his talon-like fingers, he dragged his hands toward each other in a slow, ripping motion, looking directly into the octi's eyes the whole time.

The octi looked at him.

He continued looking back.

Green light flickered, and Krork's bike ghosted onto the beach, spraying stones as it materialized fully. Krork jumped from the driver's seat.

"Whoa! Whoa! Whoa! Varrage!" Krork yelled, as he trotted closer.

Varrage relaxed his arms and paid attention to Krork, which made the octi pay attention to Krork as well.

Krork slowed to a walk, but kept his strides long, looking directly into the eyes of the purple octi, he asked: "DO YOU SPEAK?"

Krork positioned himself directly in front of the octi, between it and Varrage.

"Do you speak?" Krork repeated, fluttering his fingertips by his own mouth as if his hand were talking too.

The octi considered this for a moment, then extended several legs in a mildly sloping ramp that led to its face. A very thin leg tapped Krork in the forehead and then tapped the creature's forehead, or at least the spot between its eyes.

Krork waited a second, nodded, and started walking. When he reached the spot where the tentacles angled up from the ground, he looked once more at the creature's eyes, and seeing no reaction, no alarm, took a step on the creature's leg. Krork continued to the top, and placed his forehead against the creature's. After a moment, he closed his eyes.

Slice and Wazzi pulled up next to Varrage.

Wazzi looked where Varrage was looking, and saw Krork.

"Interesting every minute," Wazzi said.

"What do you think is happening? Are they talking?" Slice asked.

"We'll find out. Refresh your taps," Varrage answered, and the two bike pilots smacked their taps against the ground.

In time, Krork separated from the monster. He turned, and took the few steps required to reach the ground.

As Krork drew nearer to Varrage, the octi heightened to its former posture, though all its arms remained below its head.

"He is their guardian. He recognized the offensive posture of your move, and wanted to block whatever you had in mind," Krork said.

"Did you tell him it was not offense, but defense?"

Varrage looked at the creature. The creature nodded. Varrage nodded back, and the Guardian spun to return to the octi party.

Before it got halfway there, two Navy jets flew low overhead, very fast, and very loud. Every octi, including the guardian, froze and shrank and flattened. Several filled their arms with stones. The guardian rose, turning quickly to glare at Varrage.

Varrage merely faced the creature, and raised a presenting arm, hand open, to gesture at the path of the jets. He then nodded again, and the creature turned.

Krork returned to Varrage, and Varrage turned his attention to him.

"He's going to explain things to their people," Krork said. "We'll send them home one by one. Hand taps only." Krork said, and he turned to look at the scene on the beach: Huge inter-D octo-creatures dancing and making music, while humans danced, and made music right alongside them. His friend Nonstop was there too, putting on a driving show, and the Earth people were filming with their phones, and taking selfies of themselves with their friends and with the monsters, while everybody played catch with a colorful canvas bag and the sun eased lower in the sky.

"Let's go get started," Krork said, and he walked to his bike.

Krork and the others trundled slowly toward the crowd. Skyde joined them, and they formed a circle. They looked like a pit crew waiting for a race car — or a car wash team, waiting for a customer.

The purple octi moved its tentacles deliberately, and three of the dancing Octis got in a line by Krork. The first stepped into the circle. The Thrill Kings bathed it up and down with tap. Blue lights dazzled in the air. The creature turned blue, and faded home without distress. The octi erupted into fast flashes of small tentacle motions as they discussed this, and the next octi stepped into the circle.

Nonstop called out to Grace.

37

"Grace, get a shot of us!" he said as he grabbed the two octi nearest him, the magenta and the green. Standing between them, he brought them closer, until they were all standing cheek to cheek, an asparagus stalk smooshed between two cantaloupes.

Grace obliged.

After the photos, the magenta octi gently bumped foreheads with Nonstop and rose up to get in line. The green octi moved to Krork specifically, tapped him with several arms, and gently bumped foreheads with him. Krork smiled and patted the green octi, who had so successfully out-run his every move.

The purple guardian was the last to go. He locked eyes with Varrage, even as Varrage dutifully joined his tap's stream with those of his teammates. The purple octi did not bow, or nod, or bob, and neither did Varrage. The job was simply done, and then the crowd of humans cheered.

The team brought their bikes into a cluster. Skyde landed, and stored her board under the big truck bike. Grace flew her rig over to the group, but once landed, got off the bike, and stood working with her data-box.

Skyde approached her. "Want some help getting this back into the Grasshopper?" she asked, motioning to the hover bike.

"Sure," Grace answered. " In a second."

"How did it go?" Diamondsong asked her, now standing nearby, posing for selfies with the eager townspeople.

"It was fantastic," Grace said. "I have a good three minute rough-cut with some amazing shots."

"Did you save some amazing shots for yourself?" Skyde asked.

"I have two hours and forty five minutes of amazing shots. It's..." Grace looked at Varrage. "Way over an hour. Time just got away from us, I guess."

"That's because you're in field," Varrage said. "Nothing stands still in field. Everything is a rehearsal for something that will never be repeated. That's why you drill. You can at least make the smaller tasks second nature."

"You can't drill for a Bleed Zone," Nonstop said.

"No. You can't. YOU can drill for driving, and you do. You also seem to show talent regarding steering your opponent's forces."

Nonstop and Varrage both stepped to Grace's hover-bike, and joined Skyde in the pulling of latches, and the folding of frame lattices. Varrage continued his talk with Nonstop, "You should drill on your data box. You should drill on your tap. You should drill on your power tether, on elevation strategies, swamp strategies, signaling strategies..."

"Jumpin' Catfish! all right, all right. I get it. I need everything." Nonstop said.

They slid the hover frame onto the back of the Grasshopper.

"Data Box." Varrage said, walking away "If you can't do everything, make strides in one thing. Improve with your data box. Drill on its tactical inputs, drill on information-archive retrieval, drill on..."

"I feel myself shriveling," Nonstop said, turning away.

"And I'd let you. If I had the choice." Varrage said as he mounted his bike.

Varrage pointed at Slice and Wazzi, and then snapped his arm to point down the beach.

Wazzi and Slice complied, firing their bikes down the straight away. They reached ghosting speed, drove within the swirling colored lights of the forming vortex tunnel, and finally followed the plasma arc off of the planet. The crowd oohed and ahhed after the electric sizzle and pop of the ride.

"Excuse me a second." Diamondsong said to her local group of admirers. She turned to call over to Varrage. "Varrage, I have an idea. I think you need a flying rig. A great big one. One that can fire tap, and shoot out big nets."

Varrage looked at her.

"Not every set of monsters is going to be this friendly. You might need some help getting them to stand still."

Varrage kept looking at her.

"That idea has merits," he said.

She brightened.

"And it has problems," Varrage continued. "Let's discuss it with Dr. Norel back at camp."

Diamondsong fired a pretend finger gun at Varrage, and walked nearer to Grace. Talking to herself, she added: "Something that flies — that means towing it in, spare power packs..."

Nonstop called over and interrupted her.

"While you're brainstorming, let me say that I love this rig," he said, patting the Grasshopper. "It's giving me ideas."

"Great," she answered. "Talk to me when we get back. We could cook up something tasty." She stopped next to Grace and patted her on the shoulder.

"You all ready for that last step?"

"Finishing up right now."

"Do you think your idea will work?" Nonstop asked Grace. "There were a lot of people taking phone videos."

"No one has these shots. And we've got Krork talking." Grace put a flashdrive in the envelope. "And yes, I signed the release," she said, nodding to Skyde just before sealing the envelope.

Skyde walked to the back of the truck-bike, stepped up into the workbay, and walked to the handrail at the front. She smiled, and said "Great job."

Krork started the big yellow bike and began the ghost home.

"So," Nonstop said to Grace, stepping away from the Grasshopper, "You've got everything set up? Phone numbers? Everything someone will need to claim a full year of broadcast rights? Have you decided who the lucky family will be?"

"I didn't have any time to single anyone out. So... I think a Church this time. They'll at least do something good with the money."

"There's one over..." Nonstop began.

" I saw it. Yeah," Grace smiled at him and he smiled back.

"Yeah," he said.

"You ready?" Diamondsong asked Grace.

"How long will you be?" Varrage asked, standing astride his twin tailed vortex bike.

"A minute. A minute and a half." Grace answered.

Diamondsong got into the Grasshopper's driver's seat. Grace walked toward its rear.

Nonstop turned to her. She stopped, and looked at him.

"Congratulations, Grace. What you're doing is fantastic," Nonstop said, looking into her eyes and raising his hand, palm out.

"Vaptang," she said, slapping his hand very slowly.

"Vap...tamanos," he answered, smiling.

"Vap...tabulous," she answered back.

As her hand slipped slowly off his, she gave his thumb a gentle squeeze.

Her smile was wide and free and easy.

— The end —

Rik Ty

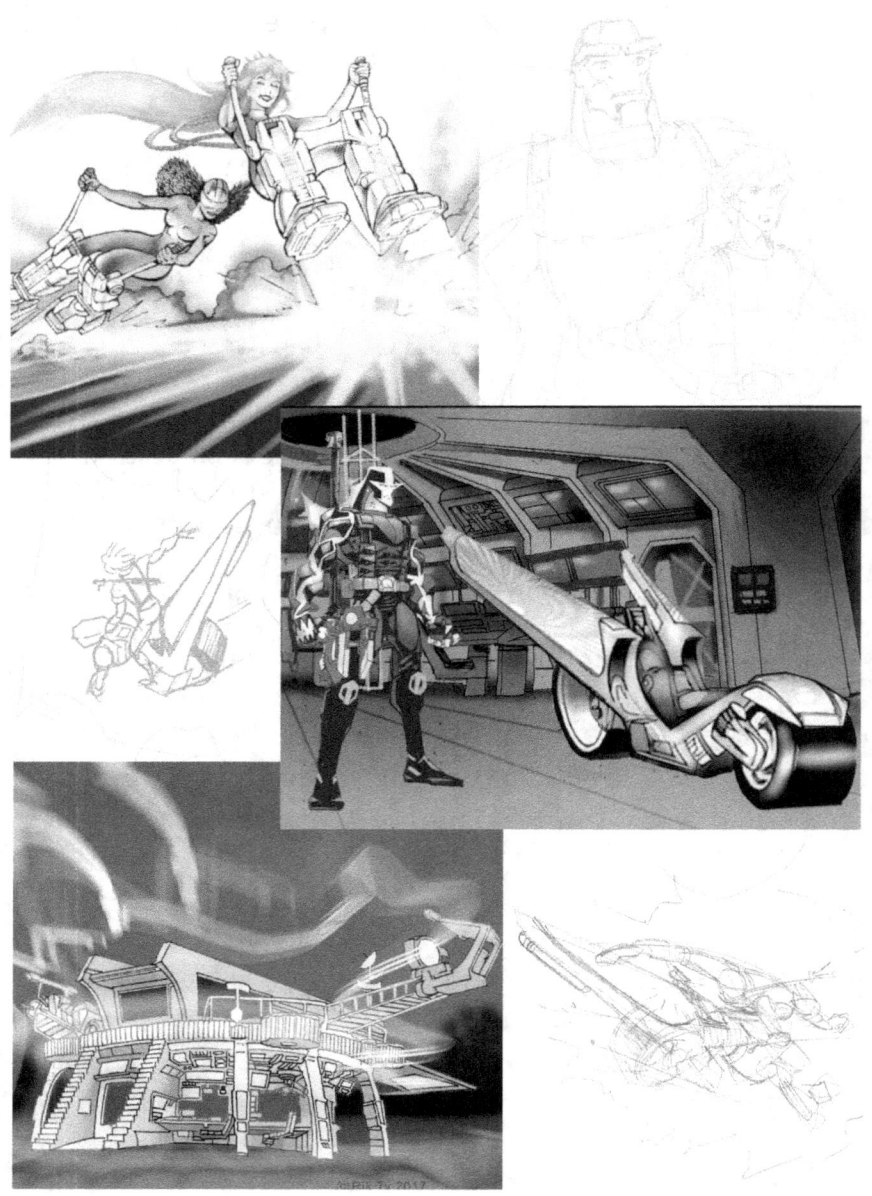

42

THRILL KINGS

The Size Of Minneapolis Upright

For Ray and Marguerite Bradbury.
And all who follow in their wake.

HONESTLY CHARLIE IT'S NOT "EAT A ITA". SHE'S IN PETA. IT'S "NEVER EAT ANYTHING WITH A FACE".

ALL ROADS ARE CLOSED. PROCEED.

AAAAAAA!

SHUT IT DOWN!

YOU WANT PEOPLE TO LISTEN TO HER OR WATCH THE DOT ON HER HEAD?

I WON'T LET ANYTHING HURT YOU.

AAAAAHH! WE'RE

IG. T.

NO, NO. REINFORCEMENTS. NO CONTACT WITH COMMAND. WELL HANDLE THIS.

NEVER READ INSTRUCTIONS? THAT'S WHY YOU HOLD CAMERAS UPSIDE DOWN.

MOV-ING MOUNTAIN.

DON'T WORRY ABOUT GETTING ME SOMEPLACE SAFE. I HAVE TO BROADCAST.

DO YOU REMEMBER THE BULLETS YOU WERE SO WEEPY ABOUT? THE ONES WITH THE EXPANDING PRONGS THAT RIPPED SUCH HUGE HOLES IN PEOPLE? THEY'RE ILLEGAL. THE ARMY WON'T USE THEM, BUT I'VE GOT A CLIP OF THEM RIGHT HERE. SPECIAL.

I... I WANT

PROMISE?

EA CTR LIEU

I HATE YOU! I HATE YOU! I HATE YOU!

IT MAY BE EVERYTHING WE'VE FEARED.

BWACK, BWACK, BWACK.

JAQUON, I WILL NOT KILL.

IT'S NOT A QUESTION OF WHAT YOU WILL KILL. IT'S A QUESTION OF WHAT YOU WILL PROTECT!

GET TV. HOW WILL I KNOW HOW THINGS TURN OUT?

CAN YOU REALLY DO THIS?

YOU ABUSED WHAT I MADE.

NO, IT LOOKS LIKE I DIDN'T GET THEM. ORRY. I DON'T HAVE THE HANG IF THIS THING YET I GUESS.

YOU'RE THINKING YOU CAN DRIVE A BUILDING?

WE DON'T DOING IT

WHAT GOOD IS A SWORD THAT ISN'T SHARP?

WE'RE DOING IT

I PUSH NOREL. I PUSH EVERYTHING I FIND. I PUSH TECHNOLOGY. I PUSH LESSER MEN.

I'M TERRIFIED TO DO IT.

I TAKE IT THAT EVERY COURTESY MEANS YOU WILL NOT STOP US FROM LEAVING?

I GET WHAT I WANT.

WE'RE GOING TO WRITE THE RULES LIEUTENANT.

WE CAN'T WIN THIS AS IT IS. WE HAVE TO SHAKE IT UP. CHANGE IT.

I DON'T HAVE TO YIELD DOCTOR. I WON.

WHAT? I'M READING THE INSTRUCTIONS.

THIS IS SHOCK RIGHT? LET'S GET YOU HOME

WHAT'S HE UP TO NOW?

I'LL TAPE IT. YOU CAN TELL IT.

Y. I CAN'T DEBOX

THE COPTER ISN'T EVEN HERE YET. DON'T GO WEAK ON ME LIEUTENANT.

I WANT ANSWERS. THE PRESIDENT IS GOING TO WANT ANSWERS. GET ME BLOCH! ALERT TESSON WE MAY NEED EVERY CHOPPER HE'S GOT.

YOU'LL DO WHAT I TELL YOU—OR I'LL KILL YOUR MEN.

CELINE PRINCESS.

IT'S WEARING US INSIGNIA.

SINGLAIR I HATE RISK. I ABHOR IT. BUT OFTEN IT IS THE RISK YOU DON'T TAKE THAT PUNISHES YOU. DO WHAT I SAY.

I CAN MAKE IT HURT. BELIEVE ME.

DADDY!

SOMETIMES YOU JUST HAVE TO INSIST. OH—OH - WHAT A BEAUTIFUL NIGHT

THRILL KINGS:

THE SIZE OF
MINNEAPOLIS UPRIGHT
Rik Ty

From the corn fields, Nonstop drove up a narrow road, past a group of red barns, and then up a small hill to another small hill. Ahead of him, the gray house sat shaded under wide trees. Funny, that with all this flat land, the owner picked the uprise to build the farmhouse on. Funny, but what did he know? He wasn't a farmer; maybe it gave you a better view. Taming all this land had to be an enormous job. If you did it, you'd have a right to feel satisfied; you'd have a right to want to sit back and gloat. Did farmers gloat? Not that he'd ever heard — but like he said, alone in his head — what did he know?

Nonstop took Rattletrap further up the road, and steadily got a closer look at the house: white trim, dark gray roof, a porch — most of which faced the road. It was a wrap around though; it also faced the fields. You could definitely come out and gloat if that's what you had a mind to do.

He heard a young girl sob: "Mommy, what are they?" and he gave the bike some juice.

He stopped on the road by the house. Looking up a long, wide driveway, he saw a family in a dooryard, rushing into a silver pickup truck filled to over-flowing with strapped-down lumber — a mother, a father, at least two young girls, a little sun-headed boy, and an orange dog. All the kids were crying hard.

"Hello," Nonstop called out, waving his arm with big friendly moves.

The boy and the dog climbed into the back of the cab. The girls stopped and stared at Nonstop — so did the father, until the father ushered the two girls and the mother into the truck. As he did, he kept his eyes on Nonstop. It was the bike. Everyone grooved on the bike — a one-wheeled disco chamber with a hot-rod-engine-robot sticking out the front end — everyone gave it their complete attention. At least on Earth. Other places, they gaped more at Nonstop himself.

The father closed the truck doors and stepped toward the rear of the truck. "Who are you? What do you know about this?"

"The creatures? You saw some creatures?"

"You're damned right we saw some creatures."

The man stopped at the back of the truck and Nonstop trundled closer, to where they could talk without yelling.

"We all saw them," the man continued, "They crawled all over our house — right over our windows." He looked at Nonstop's crazy bike. "What do you know about it?"

"Not much, but I'm here to help. I'm here to send the creatures..."

"— They're your creatures? They escaped? You made them?"

"No. They wandered here. This a Bleed Zone — like, an area of dimensional abrasion. We're here to close it up."

The farmer reached into the truck bed and put his hand on a loose two by four. "Dimensional a-"

"New science. New problems. I'm here to ask you to head out of the area for a couple of hours. You saw the little guys on your windows, but there's a big guy, and we don't know how mad he's gonna get when we start pestering him. I see you're already going, though. That's all I came to ask you to do."

The woman left the truck and stepped next to the man. "Lydia," she said to Nonstop. "Our neighbor Lydia needs help. Her truck isn't working."

The man turned to her, "The Sheriff's coming."

"He'll just bring the car."

"Then *I'll* come back for them."

"No — " the woman said, "You've got to —"

"Where's Lydia?" Nonstop asked.

The woman pointed. Nonstop turned. He saw trees — a valley too, and more hills, but primarily trees.

"She's right on the other side." The woman pointed her finger, shaking it, and then she pulled her husband back, looking up at the rooftops as she did.

"She's got a lot of foster kids," the man gestured to Rattletrap, "You're going to need more than that. . . thing."

The man guarded his wife as she got back into the truck, and then headed for the driver's side door.

Nonstop turned his bike in the driveway. "Okay, thanks," he said as the truck's big engine rumbled to life.

He waited on the road for the driver, and when the truck backed out, he signaled for the man to roll down his window. The man did, curious to hear what Nonstop had to say.

"The Bleed Zone ends here. We're at the outer edge right now. You shouldn't have any problems on the road."

The man looked at Nonstop, confused, but making the attempt to process what he'd been told.

"Thanks," he said finally, and drove off.

After that, Nonstop turned Rattletrap around and drove into the tall grass. He felt his tire grow toothy as he coasted down the grade, and was glad to know "Lydia" was a person with kids to rescue, and not the name of a favorite cow or something. Life was hard enough without trying to get a cow onto a motorcycle.

He revved up the incline on the other side of the valley. He saw lots of trees at the top of the hill. But still no house. Not yet.

He crossed a small road, went up another small hill covered with still more trees, and when the land leveled out, he made a right around the small forest, and saw the house: white, two story, dirt yard in the back, and as he got closer, he saw that the brightness of the house was solely a product of the sunlight. The house itself needed paint. Lots of it.

He approached. There was no one in the yard. There were rabbit cages, an old, dusty pickup — spotted with patches of sanded body filler. The truck looked like an old farm animal itself, a red and tan buffalo too tired to move into the shade.

He saw clothes lines — sagging with bed sheets and towels, tilting in the breeze. He saw a few tables and baskets, several ladders, a chunky plastic toy kitchen, hula hoops, and a baseball bat, lying in the dirt near the back door.

The back door had marks around it. Big dark blotches, as if someone had repeatedly thrown a wet, dirty basketball against the house — hard.

"Hello?" he called out, loud, but friendly.

No answer.

He passed the pickup. No one had driven it off the farm. Did they drive something else? Maybe.

Nonstop saw a stain under the pickup — below the engine — dark, but not wet. As he passed the machine, he saw a cardboard carton under the table nearest the truck — filled with motor-oil bottles and a plastic funnel — stashed deep under the table.

"Hello?" he called again.

One of the windows was broken. Near the basketball marks. He'd have to go in. He'd have to leave the bike and go in.

Bloch wasn't here.

There was no reason he couldn't leave the bike and go in.

Bloch wasn't here *yet*. No Army jets. No Army copters. Not yet. But the Sheriff was coming.

What could he do? Use the trees in the grass behind the house? Yeah, maybe. Maybe something else too. He saw the sheets. Chances were good that the Sheriffs of the world had seen alerts with pictures of his bike. Better that they not see it lying in a dirt yard all by itself. He rolled to the clothes lines, unpinned a sheet, and drove into the tall grass by the trees. Once he had stashed the bike and covered it with the sheet, he tried to pull the grass to cover his tracks. It didn't work well. Maybe the breeze would help.

He called "Lydia?" as he walked toward the house. Outside the door, he undocked his tap from its holster and cocked it open. The wing channels flanked his fist, and he struck their tips against the ground. They scraped a distinct mark in the dirt. Two little rectangles. Vampire teeth.

He opened the screen door, then the true door, and went in.

The kitchen seemed very dark after the sunlight.

"Hello?" He called out again, stepping in further, but hearing no answer.

A wooden hutch stood against the far wall. It held dishes and cans, and was flanked on both sides by open doorways. In front of the hutch, a wooden table stood surrounded by chairs of various styles.

The sink and stove were to his right, under a window with a curtain. He saw some cabinets, all closed. No sign of anything unusual except maybe the tall plastic cups left out on the table.

Sunlight came through the doorway on his left, and the sunlight was enough to make the adjoining room his first choice to explore. Not really a good reason, but he didn't question it. He took a few soft steps and then stood still, listening, the air as quiet as the kitchen was shaded.

The living room was a different story, plenty of light reached the room — and instantly he saw the broken window, the first in its line, with glass on the floor under its sill.

The room was neat, but crowded: two couches, two stuffed chairs, a saggy purple beanbag chair, a few ottomans, a small TV, cartoon-character lawn chairs, lots of picture books, lots of toys, most of which were lined up against the walls. Many of the larger play-things were sun-bleached — old. They shared the wall space with dozens of flat, shrink-wrapped cartons. These were printed with arched "Whittaker's Black Cherry Orchards" logos in different locations — each above a cluster of dark purple cherries. Everything seemed okay, except that the window was broken, and the toys in the middle of the room were knocked over.

As he looked around the room, he saw that it was like the outside of the house — it needed paint. Two lines of smudge marks ran along the wall behind him. Two rows of palm prints where kids changed trajectory. Two rows of smudges where kids leaned their shoulders on their ways to bed.

He walked nearer. The smudges led to the end of the white wall, to an entry hall, where there were two open bedroom doors facing him. There was light in the hall, and he could see that there was something on the floor, bright, catching the sun, a small pennant shape with a warm color, a gold, an orange, hamster-like color — it was a tail. The tip of a tail.

A noise sounded behind him, a small tink, a glass-sound. He turned to check the room, but there was nothing, just the lace curtain over the broken window, moving in the breeze. The glass shards on the floor threw back sunlight from a dozen sharp edges. He looked around the room and up the walls, where he saw more of the black stains, dry now, but once dripping.

Nothing moving, but something had been. Lydia. What happened to Lydia and her children?

"Hello," he called again. "Lydia? Are you here?"

Nothing.

He walked toward the tail in the hall.

The front door stood partially open, one half of its frame bright with sunshine. The door, dark in silhouette, nearly touched the back of the dog on the floor.

The poor dog. Orange like the one at the other house. Just like it — maybe brothers, or sisters — but this dog was dead. Lying in its own blood. Sliced. In pieces. He stepped closer. The dog's body had been sliced through the middle twice, very cleanly, around its waist and ribs, the sections still very close to each other, the organs beginning to push out from the gaps, stink rising from the violated digestive system. He saw the little dog's face. Pained. Terrified. It had been cute. It had been beautiful. Each of its forelegs had been sliced through the long bones, and the limbs had rolled as they fell. Both were in sight, inches from the rest of the animal.

Nonstop fired his tap over the dog, rippling the air around it and over it. Then over the blood pool, closing the door to make sure he didn't miss anything, not paying attention to the latching noise the door made as it locked, only looking at the animal.

Nothing happened. Nothing reacted. Nothing glowed blue.

The situation had changed, though. Killing was in the mix now. Not just running. Not just hiding. These were aggressive creatures he was dealing with. He had to check the upstairs. He'd have to check the basement too, if there was one. He stepped over the dog, skirting the blood.

The pathway up the stairs was walled and tight, barely wider than his shoulders, a cracker box built at an angle. He climbed the first step, paused to listen, and nothing happened. He took another step and the staircase creaked, but still, nothing happened. He took another step, his shoulder now at the height where something had made impact stains on the other side of the wall. He took his next step. The staircase creaked again, and this time there was an explosion of sound from the upstairs rooms — *loud*, *rapid* finger-drumming sounds, and the crash of heavy furniture hitting the floor.

Before he could get a clear idea of what was happening, the first creature rounded the doorway near the ceiling at the top of the stairs.

It was fast and it was ugly. It looked like a huge black nerve, like a Petri-dish with three weeks of black mold sprouting inside its clear center. It slapped along on legs that looked like smoke trapped in clear plastic, like raw egg white filled with streaks of rotting ink. Nonstop fired. A rush of distorted air hit the creature dead center. A second later, a second closer, and blue light enveloped the Inter-D. It vanished, revealing a flood of creatures pouring into the top of the stairwell behind it — too many, and suddenly there weren't enough seconds in the space to keep all the creatures away from him. He jumped down into the hall, slipping on the blood, but catching the stairwell wall with his elbow. He spun quickly, and as he began falling into the living room, he changed the movement into a run, clumsy at first, but then solid.

He needed more space. More space. More seconds. He turned as he ran, already firing, and as his arm extended, he was already tapping the first creature to round the staircase. It glowed blue. It vanished.

But the others kept coming, along the ceiling, along the walls, along the floor. Coming at him with whatever capabilities allowed them to slice up the dog.

Running backwards, and firing, Nonstop dashed back into the kitchen and turned, putting another doorway between himself and the creatures.

He shot the first two creatures that entered the room, but several sped in behind them, slapping along the ceiling. He side-rolled across the table, knocking the cups to the floor, and the second he cleared the table himself, a creature splatted loudly onto it — followed immediately by two more — SLAM! — SLAM! — like gunshots. Nonstop kicked the table over, grabbed a chair, and held it in front of him as backed to the sink. He fired at the three creatures on the walls — not long enough to send any of them home, but long enough to stop their advances — playing freeze tag with monsters. He repeated the action and the first creature started glowing blue. It faded and disappeared, but the three behind the table started crawling nearer. Cautiously.

He could leave through the door he came in — but then this fight would happen outside. He would be easy to surround. The walls at least kept his back protected.

He shot each of the creatures as fast as he could, though as his beam hit one, the others had time to recover and advance before getting hit by the beam again. This wouldn't work for long.

Keeping the tap firing, he dropped the chair and reached for the stove, working a dial until a rear burner lit. The creatures slowed at the fwap sound the burner made. Some stopped. Nonstop kept firing and another creature glowed blue and vanished. He spied a potholder and grabbed it off its peg. The creatures advanced. He kept firing. He stuck the potholder in the fire until it caught, instantly throwing up a column of black smoke up through the flame. He tossed the potholder onto the linoleum between him and the creatures and they slowed. The smoke detector started screeching, and the monsters turned to it, retreating a step or two from its insistent trill. Nonstop got two more creatures to vanish without having to take a step, and then it was easy getting the last two.

He listened for the drumming sound in the empty room and didn't hear it. He could try to take a haze reading with the data box, but thought against it. As he stomped the smoldering potholder, he shot the smoke alarm with his tap — out of habit, he would have supposed, and of course, nothing happened. He picked up the ruined potholder and tossed it lightly into the sink. Then he righted the table, hopping onto it to de-activate the smoke alarm. He left the spilled drinks on the floor and went to check the rest of the house for creatures or for people.

He had liked the lion-tamer feel of the chair, but didn't want to maneuver the chair around furniture or through doorways. He wanted a weapon, though, an extension of his arm that couldn't get hurt. Ambassador or not, he wanted something like a cattle-prod, something with some zap to it. Not having one was nonsense. He pulled his Voracitor blade from his gear harness. If he wasn't slashing, it was just a stick, just a length of chipped bone. But it was at least *something*. He held it out in front of him.

The living room still seemed empty. He moved a couch with his foot. Plenty of notebook pages, but no monsters. It would be a good time to take a haze reading. But he was alone. He returned to the smudged wall and kicked its base hard with the side of his foot, listening for any reaction. He passed the dog again, checked the front bedrooms, and kicked the walls a few more times.

He didn't hear anything. He didn't see anything. He went upstairs.

He didn't find anything.

It was a dresser that had fallen. It lay face down on the bare floor like a murder victim, surrounded by the million little frames and bottles and brushes that had been sitting on top of it. He righted it in one easy move as he passed. Then he walked to a bed, pulled off an old sheet, and brought it down to cover the dog.

Instead of concealing the animal, the fabric immediately starting absorbing the blood, quickly becoming saturated, and making the sight only slightly less ghastly than it had already been.

Still no people. Still no Lydia.

He'd have to come back to get the dog out of here. Did they have any rubber gloves or heavy bags in Krork's bike? He thought they had to. It was past time to take a haze reading, and if Krork were there with him, he would have suggested it. If he trusted his ability to get it right, he would have taken the reading himself. He grabbed his data-box from his harness buckle and called Krork.

"Yeah Nonstop, what's up?" Krork asked over the small machine.

"Yeah, I'm at the house," Nonstop said as he reached for the front doorknob. "Actually, I'm at a second house. The first family sent me here to help someone who doesn't have a way to get out."

Nonstop opened the door and stepped onto a front porch, outside again, facing a small road, and a yard with trees and bushes. "Anyway, I think there's someone here, but I haven't found them yet. I had a run in with the Inter-D. It went okay. I was wondering if you could take a haze reading for me — just to make sure I got them all."

"You could take a haze reading. It's easy."

"I wouldn't trust it. I could get it perfect, and I still wouldn't know for sure.

"I'll take a reading right now. You take one too, though, okay? Try at least. Get the practice."

"I will, but I'm a little busy. I'm looking for the lady. She doesn't seem to be in the house. I didn't check every inch, though, just a pass — she could be hiding.

"*Wherever* she is, she's probably hiding — or running, maybe."

"Yeah."

"Okay, I've got your reading. Good work. You're clear. Skyde got the portal, and you got the fast creatures. That's good. That just leaves big ugly. Find the lady so we can start. If you can't find her soon, we'll just have to take our chances and start anyway."

"I've got one more yard to check."

"Yeah, well —"

Nonstop turned the corner and saw a grass yard full of toys and more wash lines.

One of the sheets on the line moved in the breeze, and when it did, Nonstop saw something else.

"Wait. There's something here."

Nonstop walked quickly to the clotheslines and then around them.

He saw the back doors of an old panel truck, not very big, but yeah, pretty old, sticking out of a hill. A buried truck. It looked like someone just drove it into the Earth.

"Yeah, yeah, Krork, I think I'm looking at a storm cellar."

"In the yard? Not under the house? I must be thinking of the wrong word."

"Yeah, yeah, no, you're right. A cellar is usually under a house. But they sometimes put tornado cellars in the yard. In case the house gets knocked down — Is Missouri tornado country?"

"You're asking the wrong guy. I only heard of Missouri a half hour ago."

"Yeah, it must be, though. They buried a whole truck. It's wild, you should see it, just the back of it is sticking out."

"Send me a data-stream."

Nonstop ignored the request, and continued speaking, taking a step closer to the truck. "Yeah, it's got a vent pipe on the top — it's been here a while; the hill is covered with grass, edges are sealed up with tar. Alright, hold on, I'll call you back."

"Hello?" Nonstop called out as he re-docked his data-box.

He reached for the latch handle on the right hand door. The windows of the truck were intact, but so dirty he couldn't see inside them.

"Hello?" He knocked on the metal door, turned the latch handle, and there, huddled in the rear of the little cave, were Lydia and her kids. Nonstop's first impression was of a dozen sets of white eyes, practically glowing in the shadowed space. He saw them, even at the same time he watched the huge kitchen knife the terrified woman pointed at him.

"Who are" — the woman started to say, and Nonstop took a step back.

"Lydia? Hello, my name is Nonstop. I'm here to take you to town."

The knife blade danced in the air as the woman looked back and forth between Nonstop and the space beyond his shoulders. She swung her free arm across the group of children. "What's going on? What's — We saw monsters — We."

"I know. I know. I just got rid of the ones that were here. I sent them back where they came from. How many are you? You can come out, Nonstop started to count, "One, two,"

"We're staying right here."

"You can stay in the truck for now if you want," Nonstop nodded. "I only have a bike; it can only take three of you at a time — maybe five — I have to get a different rig, so I can take you into town, or into the hills, or someplace."

"What's happening? What is this? What's going on?"

"Truth? You guys are in an interdimensional Bleed Zone. I'm here to take you out of it so we can close things up and get them back to normal." Nonstop stepped away from the truck but left the doors open. "You can come out. My partner just took a reading, and this area is clear."

The kids started to move, but the woman pushed them back.

"If its clear, why do you want to take us to town?"

"There's a big guy out in the field, about the size of Minneapolis standing upright — big and mad and walking around. It's going to take a while to send him back, and once we start, he's likely to get super-mad." Nonstop looked over his shoulder. "That red truck over there doesn't work, does it?"

"Not now. Mr. Johansso . . . No. Not now."

Nonstop turned back to Lydia and the kids. "Johansson? Is that the family across the road? They sent me here to get you. They're heading into town, but the back of their truck was full of wood. They didn't have any room. He might try to come back for you. We might pass him on the road. How many are you in there?"

"We're twelve altogether. Were you in the house? Did you see a dog?" Lydia took a step out into the sun. At some point, she had lowered the knife, but Nonstop hadn't noticed.

"I saw the dog," Nonstop said, shaking his head, "I'm sorry, It's not good news."

It could have been a kid. It could have been a kid. Itcouldhavebeenakid.

Lydia looked at the house, and the yard, and at Nonstop, and crossed her chest with her knife arm, gripping the weapon tightly. Her hands and her shoulders shook. The children started leaking out of the truck, stepping into the sun — a surprising mix of sizes and skin colors. One boy held a baseball bat, a small girl carried some kind of bladed garden hoe.

"Don't go too far," Lydia told them, "In case we have to run back in."

The boy with the bat stepped around Lydia and stared at Nonstop, followed by another child and the small girl with the garden spear. None of them raised their weapons; they just kept wandering closer to Nonstop. One small girl stepped nearer to Lydia, and Lydia stooped to pick her up, deftly spinning the knife handle in her fingers so that the blade hung loosely and away from the child. She brought the girl to her shoulder and rocked her.

"Wow. You've got a big family." Nonstop said.

"Childhood won't wait. All right. Get us out of here. Take us to town."

A boy stepped closer to Lydia and rubbed the back of the tiny girl in her arms.

"Yeah, let me set it up," Nonstop worked at his data-box. The trio of kids moved right next to him.

"What's your name?" the black-haired boy with the bat asked.

"Nonstop," Nonstop said, poking the screen of his data-box.

"Nonstop is your name?"

"Nonstop is your name?" The small girl asked too.

"Nonstop is my apelido — my riding name. Everyone calls me Nonstop. What's your name?"

"I'm George," the black-haired boy said.

"I'm Ralphie-J," his brother said.

"I'm Cynthia," the little girl said.

"Really? I have a very good friend named Cynthia. Pleased to meet you."

A voice crackled over the data box: "Yeah, Nonstop?"

"Hi Krork, I've got twelve people to take out, mostly kids. Will your bike fit them?"

"Sure, I could crowd in twelve kids."

"Eleven kids, one adult. Okay, here's the thing. I want to switch bikes with you — the lady is freaked out. I don't want her to see you 'cause - you know, she'll think you're a monster."

"You know, my mother thinks I'm very good looking. On the other hand, she would throw up if I brought you home to dinner."

"Oh. Nice. Is that how she cooks? She throws up, then we all grab spoons?"

"Ack. Why do I even talk to you?"

"Okay, I take it back. If you see your mother, please tell her to have a lovely day. You ghosting?"

"Yes. I have the reading."

"Not here, though. Undershoot a little — closest side of the house."

"Okay. Be right there."

Nonstop lowered the data —

"Your friend is a monster?" George asked, close again.

"Well, he's not a monster, but he is weird looking. Here."

Nonstop finished docking the data-box, then dug in his gear harness. He pulled a printout from a pouch and showed it to the kids.

"Handsome, right?" The kids bent over the picture.

"Vehement," Ralphie-J said.

"Yeah, vehement!" George agreed.

"Vehement?" Nonstop asked himself.

"I want to see," Cynthia said, muscling her way between the two boys. "Ooooo," she added, "He's yellow?"

"Yeah. He's got skin like a lemon. A lot of it. He's real big."

"He looks like an action figure. Like a dinosaur," George said.

"I'll tell him you said that."

A spasm of green light played across the dirt by their feet, though the source had come from the side of the house, the same side Nonstop had approached first.

"He's here, would you like to meet him?"

The kids jumped, crying "Yeah! Yeah! Vehement!"

"All right," Nonstop took a step, the kids following him immediately. "You stay out here where your Mom can see you, okay?" Nonstop stirred the air with his hand to indicate the general area, and then turned the corner and saw Krork stepping off his bike — a 5-wheeled mini-dump truck with a fat recumbent motorcycle in place of a cab, also yellow, like its driver.

"You've got some fans," Nonstop said.

Krork stood near the bike and waved to the kids.

They jumped up and down and yelled "Vehement" over and over. Krork grinned. "Where's the bike?", he said.

"What bike?"

"Your bike. The bike I'm supposed to drive back into the Bleed Zone."

"Oh right. Its over there by those trees, under a sheet."

"So the woman's going to see me anyway."

"You'll be walking away. I'll ride the bike out and you walk behind it and then just keep going. Wave. Say 'Hi'."

Nonstop waved the kids back, and punched in the start code on the big bike. It purred quietly and he rolled it forward. Krork walked alongside it, waved hello, and the kids and their mother all gasped.

"It's okay. He's my friend," Nonstop called out. "We have to get going. Climb in the back."

George started to run in. Nonstop raised a hand. "Wait for your Mom," he said.

Lydia approached cautiously, children clouding behind her as if she had magnetic pull. Nonstop stepped off the bike and asked her where the nearest town was. She told him, and started to give directions, but he asked her to just point.

Krork rode Rattletrap down the hill, looking ridiculous on the human sized machine. He began his ghost run, and colors fanned in the air behind him. The kids began shouting, and when the arc-gate sizzled and Krork faded away into a green haze, they jumped up and down and screamed "Did you see that?" at each other.

"Alright, come on. Get on," Nonstop said to the crowd. "On the top of the walls there's a railing. Move the knapsacks around until you have something to hold on to. I'm going to take it easy. But make sure you hold on to something. Lydia, please take the last spot and watch. . ."

Lydia nodded, way ahead of him.

He watched them get on and find hand holds, and he looked over their heads down to the farmland — wide enough to see a rain cloud pouring out next to a sun-patch. He found himself thinking of tornadoes. What would one look like down there on the plain? What must the early people have thought? It would have to have seemed like a monster — or the wrath of G*d — or some other spirit-world entity. The air is angry — it has to seem like something is mad.

It has to seem like monsters.

"Okay," Nonstop said, walking toward the front of the bike. "You're going to see a lot of crazy lights. You can yell if you want, you can scream if you want — but you can't let go. Right? — like a rollercoaster."

"Scream?" Lydia asked.

"Like a rollercoaster — like the coolest one ever." He looked at Cynthia, "The most vehement."

Cynthia smiled and looked away.

Nonstop got on the bike and trundled it from the dirt and onto the grass, rolling downhill then, toward the road.

He looked into the field again; the last chance before they left up the roadway, hit 88, and then hit the wild realm-lines. Once in a lifetime for these kids, maybe. Depending on how things went, maybe not; maybe these kids would be vortex bus drivers, or bike pilots like himself — depending on how things went.

Over the fields he could see Skyde, a tiny white dot flying in the air. He couldn't see Varrage.

But the whole gasping bike-load could see the Inter-D — big as a ten story building, looking like a hill itself, its back and shoulders covered with something that looked like trees. It moved slowly, purposelessly, silent from distance.

In a few minutes that would change. And a few minutes after that, it would change again, and the creature would be home. And then *everyone* would be home, where the porch is waiting for you to sit, and look out at the field,

and know you had done a good day's work.

- The end -

A 100 Word THRILL KING ADVENTURE By Rik Ty

"SNOW"

The tentacled giant slid on the small avalanche, crashing through fir and pine before toppling the chalet and mangling the first tower of the lift. Customers screamed and fled, adding color to the riot. Nonstop pursued full speed on his vortex bike, following the creature even as it crashed through the protective fencing and plummeted into the gorge.

Falling through blue sky, and unsure how the creature's momentum would translate across worlds, Nonstop fired and sent it home. Then he looked at the rocks a thousand feet below and thought of his impact diffusion.

This would be an excellent test.

Rik Ty

A 100 Word THRILL KING ADVENTURE
By Rik Ty

"ADORABLE"

Nonstop was about to leave the basement of Outpost 14 when he heard a noise. Behind him, the long hallway stood empty except for a doorway that hadn't been there before -- the same heavily framed bulkhead he had just left it seemed. He took a few more steps and heard the doorway sliding along the wall behind him.

"Sta-ay," he said sternly, wagging his finger. The doorway looked at him sadly.

He continued on, passing blossoming quantum storerooms, with the doorway following, and knew, that if he didn't hurry, he was going to wind up right back where he started.

A 100 Word THRILL KING ADVENTURE By Rik Ty

"THE CREVASSE"

A wall of insects blocked off the crevasse, creating an animated mosaic of a long clawed, buzzing monster with jagged teeth. Arriving, Krork called "Wait!" to Nonstop, and then called out to the crevasse in the Inter-D's own language: ["JOLANT. SPEAKS. WE FRIENDS. WE SEND HOME."]

"You spoke to them?" Nonstop asked, as the mosaic devoured a crude depiction of him.

"Yes," ["WE SEND HOME,"] Krork repeated. The mosaic slowly rearranged into an archway, and cautiously, Nonstop entered. Krork Followed.

The buzzing archway matched their every step, threatening to lower at their first mistake, and fill their lungs with insects.

A 100 Word THRILL KING ADVENTURE
By Rik Ty

"FIVE WRENCHES"

The spatial anomaly was five phase iterations from defeating Nonstop's tap and thus kaleidoscopically devouring the Earth inside a thousand-year black collapsing.

Nonstop had been late to the Bleed Zone, trying to get a fifth wrench to land in a plastic bucket, but as it was, his hand was in the right spot, at the right angle, at exactly the right moment to fire his tap and avert disaster -- though he never knew it. Instead, he apologized to his team for being late again, and helped complete the mission.

We never fully know,
how many trucks don't hit us.

Afterworks

About Not So Bad

About The Size Of
Minneapolis Upright

About The Thrill Kings

About The Author

ABOUT NOT SO BAD

Not So Bad is the first story I've written that specifically takes place after the events of Fragmented Sky, and it has had an odd genesis. I've had several sketches and story ingredient notions building up that I assumed I would use in the next major Thrill Kings novel — such as a new, simpler bike idea, similar to Rattletrap, but one that puts the active emphasis on the human in the drawing. Also, a bit of an emotional separation between Grace and Nonstop — not a split, but space enough for work, and most importantly, the idea I've been itchy to use for years: the awarding of mission footage to needy people. This is an idea I've been holding since the fax machine days (early 90's) in a different entertainment storyline ("Boom-bastic Bazooka BoyZ"). I doubted I was ever going to get around to using it with Bazooka BoyZ, but I loved the idea, and wanted to give it to Thrill Kings. It's a big idea. It deserved a full dramatization, but I didn't know when I was going to write a follow up novel, so I thought it was time to use it in a story. A dramatic use of the idea can come in the future (probably not, since the cat is out of the bag).

Those are SOME of the elements that pushed the story forward. But here is the main one:

Right before Christmas, my wife and I did some shopping in a mall. The mall was not crowded, but it DID have shoppers. While my wife stepped into Macy's, I paced an empty spot outside the store and did some thinking. While I did, I watched the passing shoppers, and I asked myself "What would THEY need to know about Thrill Kings? What sets it apart from the 100,000 other works of Heroic fiction screaming for their attention?" I thought, "Well, the group fights monsters, but the tone isn't always dire.

Sometimes the Thrill Kings have a good time WHILE they are fighting the monsters." That seemed like a good element to stress the next chance I got.

To me. the MOST standard symbol of inter-dimensional monstrousness is the tentacled creature — Cthulhu from Lovecraft, Kang from the Simpsons, Flying Spaghetti Monsters from internet memes, etc. So an image came to my mind that was somewhat similar to the cover I managed to paint, and I set to work developing a story that would justify the cover. I think it is a very thin story, but being light and breezy was part of the tone I was chasing. I didn't expect to riff on personal concentration, and mental bandwidth, but it emerged anyway.

Having fun with tentacled monsters in a short piece, was greatly helped by having tentacled creatures who had good attitudes — creatures that might be more interested in dancing with their neighbors than killing them. Now, if dancing Octopi appeal to you, Have I got good news. I've been following the facebook posts of J. S. Burke since last summer. She is always finding fun, and amazing things to post about nature, and often about octopi. I just read her novel "The Dragon Dreamer" (My review is on Amazon). It features a Dragon named Arak, and an amazing octopus character named Skree. If you enjoyed seeing octopus-ish creatures swinging from trees and bopping to speaker pods, give the Dragon Dreamer a chance (no speaker pods). Burke's octopus community is richly developed — they dance, they make communicative pictograms on their skins using controllable pigment cells, they decorate their dens with colored lichen, they farm, analyze chemicals, make peace, make art, make fantastic origin stories — all miles and miles above anything you'll see in this story. I ESPECIALLY recommend her books if you have children just about to read on their own. She doesn't write childrens' books; she writes upbeat fantasy, but still, you couldn't do better.

I think that's it. I'll see you next time. It might be Sparrows and Hawks (Grim, unwritten), it might be "Ralph's Summer Day" (Absurd) (but at least it's written), or "Wizard War at Burning Man" (a possible Thrill King entry into a Space Fantasy anthology, unwitten), or "A Small Amount Of Occupied Space" (written, Nonstop and Krork sit on the side of a cliff, and discuss their own crackpot theories regarding how they can possibly digest food, that according to their own realities, doesn't actually exist), or it might be something else. Who knows? But I'll see you then!

- end -

ABOUT THE SIZE OF MINNEAPOLIS UPRIGHT

Two things inspired me to develop this story and see it through to completion. I wanted to make sure that at least one of these Thrill Kings projects covered the basics of a Bleed Zone mission — before I told more involved stories, where the specifics of the Bleed Zone drove the plot. In this piece, there is a nest of pee wee monsters. A little hunting, a little running, a little tapping, and then the problem is over. Making that model more interesting, is at least a starting point for future stories. For instance, in the next adventure (The Gray Walls), a Bleed Zone has Krork and Nonstop hunting an Inter-D that seems to devour patches of continuums, or perhaps ENTIRE continuums for its nutrition. Worse, the team begins to suspect that their own specific patch of continuum has already been eaten — with them in it. That problem is more specific than pee wee monsters, and might be easier to enjoy if the reader is already familiar with the basic mission model.

The second element that pushed the story forward was the idea of the buried truck as storm cellar. I've never seen one personally, but they exist, and I love the idea. It's ingenious.

Interestingly, my favorite part of this story (and it is my favorite by far) is the whole "vehement" section, and that was made up on the spot. I am a plotter with an appreciation for pantsing — first you build a stage, and then you dance on it. I'm a clumsy dancer, I may step on your toes, but I hope you'll join me for future turns 'round the floor.

See you next time,

-Rik

ABOUT THE THRILL KINGS

The Thrill Kings are an Interdimensional Rescue Team.

Without going into too much detail, here are some back-story elements that you might like to know: Interdimensional travel was invented by a scientist named Edmond Norel. Wheeled vehicles work best, wheeled vehicles with external riders, work best of all.

Dr. Norel has assembled close to 100 trusted people to assist him in developing the technology.

A string of catastrophes brought us to where we are today:

First, A team of riders were stranded on a hostile alien world. Most of the riders, and those sent to rescue them, were killed. Those that managed to return, returned dimensionally wounded.

Later, Colonel Bloch, a secretive weapons procurer with past ties to Dr. Norel, broke down the doors of Dr. Norel's research facility, and tried to commandeer the project Norel was working on. That project happened to be interdimensional technology, and Norel and his teams used it to escape. They now live nomadically, off-realm, and continue their work.

Shortly after Norel's teams escaped the Colonel, abrasion points began erupting across the realm-lines (primarily on Earth). These abrasion points featured areas where elements of one dimension were pulled through to another. If unanswered, these eruptions would allow direct gravitational recognition between both dimensions, and threaten the life-giving orbits of all involved worlds.

Norel could run from the Colonel, but he couldn't let the abrasion points go unanswered. The four riders who returned from the alien world, all show signs of impact diffusion (the greater the impact, the greater the diffusion — at least seemingly). The limits are untested, but these four riders, who each have their own ideas on how to solve problems, are who Dr. Norel can send to repair the Bleed Zone eruptions on Earth — impact diffusion is critical, because Colonel Bloch still wants to steal the technology, and returning home, will mean facing gunfire.

These four riders will confront the unknown.

These four riders will HAVE to prevail.

These four riders will have to be Thrill Kings.

(The youngest rider's term, NOT Dr. Norel's.)

- end -

From Amazon Reviews of
Thrill Kings: Fragmented Sky

"The pace of this novel is unreal! I loved it", "Honestly, I pride myself on fast pace and this is like a benchmark for action stories! I couldn't be more impressed.",

"Slick, quick paced, fun and colorfully detailed (literally)",

"it's seldom such works of depth and complexity which are also lots of fun come around",

The book's a little on the long side, and might be slightly overwhelming for those just stepping into this world, but it's a wonderful introduction to the characters and concepts. Definitely recommended.

"Suddenly, in the middle section of the book everything came together and I got swept up in the plot and the world and finished the last half of the book in one sitting. It closes with climatic, world-shaking events and delivers a thrill on every page."

***

Why not add your review?

ABOUT THE NOVEL

Thrill Kings: Fragmented Sky is the final act in the grand battle between Dr. Norel and Col. Bloch. It reveals who will control Vortex technology, and if its existence will remain secret or be announced to the world. The stakes raise far beyond that, and the book's thunderous climax reveals whether reality can continue to exist at all. Big risks. Big action. Big fun.

This is a GIANT novel, full of fantastic moments. The story takes place on one Summer night, and has all the elements that make such a night so wonderful: the moon, a little romance, monsters, nightmare weaponry, fast motorcycles, aliens, weird physics, psychedelic-interdimensional-driving-vistas, and general-end-of-existence cataclysm.

Easily, the best first date you'll ever read.

ABOUT THE AUTHOR

Rik Ty is a cartoonist and toy designer living in New York. He is married, and has wonderful children. He gets more and more nearsighted everyday, and may soon start applying paint directly with his eyeball. (Blending is blinking - wink, wink!)

THANK YOU

Thank you,
I'd love to know your reactions to the stories. Please leave a review, tell your friends, and help the project grow!

Thank you,
-Rik Ty

You can sign up for the newsletter to get all major announcements at:
http://www.thrillkingsnow.com/cast-1-1/

Visit the Rik Ty facebook page for more freebies, and day to day news.

The nice thing about print books is that they are independent objects. They are not constantly updated and changed. With that in mind, and knowing that there is no telling WHEN you're reading this — it might be good to see what is happening with Thrill Kings currently. You can check:
Thrill Kings Now.com (lowercase, one word)
The Rik Ty facebook page,
The Amazon Author Page.
https://www.amazon.com/author/rikty

and soon to be instagram etc.

Thanks again!

I'll leave you with a freebie. There are 6 DELUXE excerpts from Fragmented Sky available **FREE** for you to explore. Each is complete. Each is a cool Thrill Kings set-piece that starts, develops, and finishes. Now that you know some of the characters, these will all be fun! Available as ebooks on **KOBO.com,** and as PDFs on **Thrill Kings Now.com** (I'd personally prefer you use Kobo, since they will give a tally, and you can leave reviews). Tell your friends! Thank You!